Jobs People Do

Rubbish Collectors

by Emily Raij

raintree

a Capstone company — publishers for children

Raintree is an imprint of Capstone Global Library Limited, a company incorporated in England and Wales having its registered office at 264 Banbury Road, Oxford, OX2 7DY – Registered company number: 6695582

www.raintree.co.uk
myorders@raintree.co.uk

Edited by Gena Chester
Designed by Kyle Grenz
Original illustrations © Capstone Global Library Limited 2021
Picture research by Jo Miller
Production by Spencer Rosio
Originated by Capstone Global Library Ltd
Printed and bound in India

978 1 3982 0316 7 (hardback)
978 1 3982 0315 0 (paperback)

British Library Cataloguing in Publication Data
A full catalogue record for this book is available from the British Library.

Acknowledgements
We would like to thank the following for permission to reproduce photographs:
Alamy: Cultura Creative, 1, Jim West, 10, Richard Levine, 21; Dreamstime: Auremar, Cover; Getty Images: Carnegie Museum of Art/Teenie Harris Archive/Contributor, 28; iStockphoto: PeopleImages, 12, TexasPixelPro, 5, USGirl, 19, vm, 9; Shutterstock: Africa Studio, 14, Johnny Habell, 15, 17, Joshua Resnick, 7, Kzenon, 13, MAHATHIR MOHD YASIN, 25, MakDill, 20, Nick Beer, 22–23, Rob Crandall, 11, SeventyFour, 27, vadim kozlovsky, 26, Yaroslav Sabitov, 8

Contents

Words in **bold** are in the glossary.

What is a rubbish collector?

Yuck! What's that smell? It's the kitchen rubbish. The bag is full and stinky. It can go in the dustbin outside. Your neighbours put out their bins too. But who picks up all that rubbish? Who takes it away? Rubbish collectors! They keep our communities clean and safe.

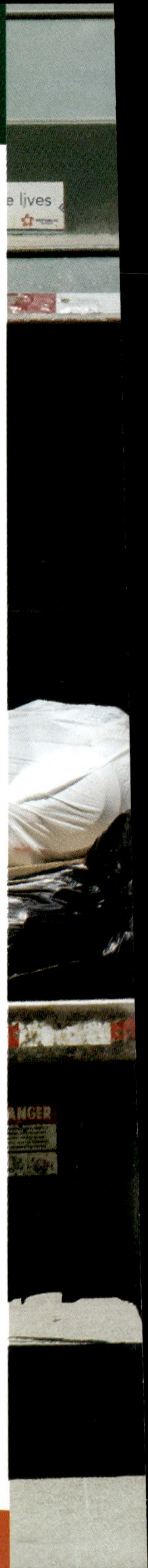

People in the UK throw away £13 billion worth of food each year. That is a lot of rubbish!

Other types of rubbish include paper, plastic, metal, glass and garden waste. Some rubbish is **electronic**, such as computers and TVs.

A lot of rubbish ends up in **landfills**. Some is burned, which can make the air dirty. We can **recycle** a lot of our rubbish instead.

Where rubbish collectors work

Rubbish collectors use big lorries. They pick up rubbish in villages, towns and cities and take it to waste **transfer** stations.

The rubbish is taken off the lorries. Then it is weighed. It gets sorted. Other workers pull out things that can be recycled. The rubbish is pressed down. This makes it smaller. Now more rubbish can go to landfills at one time.

Some collectors drive their lorries straight to the landfill. They dump the rubbish. It gets pressed down and covered with soil.

Our rubbish can be sorted so that items such as paper, glass and plastic can be picked up for recycling.

What rubbish collectors do

Rubbish collectors may work alone. But they can work in groups of two or three. One worker drives the lorry.

One or two workers ride on the back of the lorry. The lorry moves slowly through streets. Cars may be parked on the road. Drivers need to remember **routes** and watch out for cars, people and animals.

Most collectors do not need to lift the bins. They put them in place and then a rear **loader** picks them up from the road.

Other lorries have front loaders. Those pick up big dumpsters. They are outside big buildings and businesses. Some lorries have a packer blade. It presses the rubbish down to make room for more rubbish.

Some lorries do not have rear or front loaders. Some have a **mechanical** arm. The arm lifts the bins. Then it dumps the rubbish. Rubbish falls into the **hopper**.

Other bin lorries do not have an arm. These lorries need teams of collectors. Rubbish collectors pick up the bins and dump the contents into the lorry. Collectors have to get each bin. It is hard work. It's smelly too.

Rubbish is collected on a certain day of the week. Household rubbish is collected separately from recycling and garden waste. People usually have special bins for each type of rubbish. If not, rubbish is put into bags.

Collectors check that they have taken all the rubbish. They pick up any items of rubbish that fall into the road. At the end of their day, collectors clean their lorry.

Rubbish collectors work in all weathers. They are out in the heat and cold. Bad weather can make their job harder. It is hard to see in heavy rain. It is hard to drive in heavy snow.

In some countries, bin lorries have snowploughs. These are like big shovels on the front of lorries. They clear the roads. Workers move snow instead of picking up rubbish. They make the roads safe. Then collectors must pick up the rubbish that wasn't collected during the bad weather.

Some rubbish collectors work six days a week. They get rubbish from all the places on their route. This may take 10 to 18 hours. Some start early in the morning. Others work all night.

The work can be **dangerous**. Sharp objects can poke through rubbish bags. Collectors can get cut. Sometimes rubbish flies off the packer blade. Rubbish can hit collectors. They also have to watch for cars. Collectors could get hit.

To stay safe, rubbish collectors wear special clothes. The clothes have **reflective** tape. This helps drivers see workers in the street. Collectors wear gloves. The gloves protect their hands. Boots protect their feet.

Some collectors wear hats, goggles and masks. Hats protect their heads. Goggles protect their eyes. Masks keep out bad smells.

reflective tape
足立800
25-15

How to become a rubbish collector

Some rubbish collectors need a special driving licence. Then they can use the equipment on the lorry. Collectors may need to pass a special driving test too.

Safety is very important. Rubbish collectors must know how to safely lift heavy bins. The lorry drivers need to be careful and good with directions.

Some workers pick up dangerous materials. They may find chemicals. Workers must know how to get rid of the materials safely.

Famous rubbish collectors

Many people made rubbish collection easier. George Dempster changed how we pick up rubbish. In 1935, he created the Dempster Dumpster. It could be picked up and emptied easily by machines.

John Arwood started National Garbage Man Day in the United States in 2011. It is now called Waste & Recycling Workers Week.

a Dempster Dumpster

Fast facts

- **What rubbish collectors do:**
They keep our communities clean and safe.

- **Key types:**
lorry drivers, rubbish collectors, recycling collectors, street sweepers

- **Key tools:**
mechanical arm, hopper, packer blade, rear loader, sweeper, snowplough

- **Key clothes:**
gloves, boots, hat, goggles, mask

- **Education needed:**
sometimes a special driving licence, tests

- **Famous rubbish collectors:**
George Dempster, John Arwood

Glossary

dangerous likely to cause harm or injury

electronic powered by electricity; electricity is a form of energy

hopper storage area in a bin lorry

landfill place where rubbish is buried

loader machine that lifts and carries loads

mechanical operated by a machine or machinery

recycle make used items into new products; people can recycle items such as paper, glass, plastic and aluminium

reflective throwing back light

route road or course followed to get somewhere

transfer move from one place to another

Find out more

Books

How Effective is Recycling? (Earth Debates), Catherine Chambers (Raintree, 2016)

This Book is Not Rubbish: 50 Ways to Ditch Plastic, Reduce Rubbish and Save the World!, Isabel Thomas (Wren & Rook, 2018)

What a Load of Rubbish! What Happens To The Things We Throw Away? (The Story of Sanitation), Riley Flynn (Raintree, 2019)

Website

www.dkfindout.com/uk/science/materials/recycling-materials
Find out more about recycling materials.

Index